Isabella,

Thanks for comming

to my birthday

Party

Love, Paris

Special thanks to Rebecca Dolgin for all her fashion tips

A GOLDEN BOOK • NEW YORK

BARBIE and associated trademarks and trade dress are owned by, and used under license from, Mattel, Inc.
Copyright © 2007 Mattel, Inc. All Rights Reserved.
Published in the United States by Golden Books, an imprint of Random House Children's Books, a division of Random House, Inc., New York, and in Canada by Random House of Canada Limited, Toronto. No part of this book may be reproduced or copied in any form without permission from the copyright owner. Golden Books, A Golden Book, and the G colophon are registered trademarks of Random House, Inc.

Library of Congress Control Number: 2006935782
ISBN: 978-0-375-83548-3
www.goldenbooks.com   www.randomhouse.com/kids

MANUFACTURED IN CHINA

10 9 8 7 6 5 4 3 2 1

Check out Barbie® online! www.barbie.com℠

Barbie™

Cool & Casual

By Mary Man-Kong

Interior design by Elana Davidian
Cover photography by the Mattel Photo Studio
Interior photography by Willy Lew, Shirley Fujisaki,
Julia Raylow, Doug Elliston, Steve Toth, and Judy Tsuno

Ding-dong! Barbie answered the door and was surprised to see her friend Teresa.

"Help!" Teresa cried to Barbie. "I finally got invited to Lily's party—but I have nothing to wear! I could use a whole new wardrobe. Do you think you can help me?"

"Don't panic," Barbie replied. Teresa was usually shy, so Barbie was glad that her friend had reached out to her for help. "All you need are a few basic pieces. Why don't we go to the mall tomorrow and see what we can find there?"

"Thanks, Barbie!" exclaimed Teresa. "You're a lifesaver!"

"I think your everyday wardrobe should be cool and casual to match your personality," Barbie suggested when she met Teresa at the mall. "Let's start by getting you some pants. These flared jeans look great. I also love pants that have trendy designs or hip extras like colorful buttons or pretty tassels."

"What do you think of these?" asked Teresa.

"Those are awesome!" Barbie exclaimed. "I like the silver buttons on the gray pants and I love how soft the brown pair feels."

Dress It Up

Make casual classy. Try a crisp shirt, a ruffle-sleeve top, or a pretty sweater with sequins or embroidery to dress up pants or jeans.

me
me
me

cool store!

"You can also experiment with different pant lengths," Barbie said as she spotted a pair of capris and tried them on to show Teresa.

"What do you think?" asked Barbie as she stepped out of the dressing room.

"Those are so cute!" replied Teresa. "And I love the pink top you chose, too."

Cool

love ya!

xoxo

yeah TOTALLY

Pants Rule!

- Pinstripe patterns make you appear taller.

- If you're tall, try cropped pants. Wear them with flat shoes or boots.

Pink Is my Favorite

"To really make a fashion statement, you can layer your look," suggested Barbie as she stepped out of the dressing room. "You can wear jeans and a sweater dress and layer it with a short cropped denim jacket. What do you think?"

"I'll take it!" said Teresa. "And look at these other jackets I found."

"Those are perfect," replied Barbie. "They'll work well with your new pants. Your closet will be filled in no time!"

girly girl

Love It!

one busy superSTAR

Cool Colors

- Try similar tones: tan with chocolate brown, pink with deep raisiny brown, or gray with black.

- Mix colors that complement each other: gray with rose or teal, yellow with brown, pink with orange, or royal blue with black.

Rock your Style !!!

At the SuperStyle store, Barbie spotted her friend Stephanie and waved.

"Hey, Barbie," called Stephanie. "What are you up to?"

"I'm helping my friend Teresa with a fashion makeover," replied Barbie. "Can you give her any advice?"

"I love to wear bright colors so that I stand out," said Stephanie.

"I see what you mean," said Teresa. "I love your red shirt against those yellow pants. And that bag rocks!"

"Thanks!" Stephanie replied. "Good luck with your makeover."

B Girly

one
busy
superSTAR

Mix and Match

• If your top and bottom are solid colors, pair up colors that complement each other, such as brown and powder blue.

• If one piece of clothing has a pattern, match it with a solid that picks up a color in that pattern.

• Feeling brave? Go for the three-color rule and mix a new color into an outfit. For example, if a skirt has green and blue flowers, add a third color by wearing a yellow top.

Call friends

The next day, Barbie went shopping with Teresa at her favorite shoe store, Twinkle Toes. "Now, let's see what we can find for you," Barbie said. "A pair of ankle boots will look chic with all the clothes you've already picked out."

"I love your knee-high boots, too," Teresa commented. "Are they comfortable?"

"Don't worry," Barbie said with a laugh. "These boots were made for walking— and *shopping*!"

Shoes, Shoes, Shoes!

- For straight-leg "stovepipe" pants, go with ankle boots or peep-toe shoes.

- If the pants have a slight flare, choose closed-toe wedges or ballerina flats.

- For skirts, try knee-high boots.

So Cute

Over the next few weeks, Teresa often stopped by Barbie's house for help. Barbie didn't mind. She loved giving her friend fashion tips.

"Here's a new outfit that I just got," Barbie said. "Hoodies are fun—and functional if it rains. And I like to add a funky chunky necklace to make the look totally me!"

"Fabulous!" Teresa said.

"Time to accessorize!" exclaimed Barbie. "Let me change, and then we can find a cute bag to go with your outfits."

Natural Bling

- Chunky jewelry and accessories made of natural materials, such as wood, shells, and coral, will give your outfit some flair.

you make me laugh

meet at the mall

girly girl

At Fashion Accessories, there were so many bags that Teresa didn't know where to start.

"I think this tan bag would work best. It's compact and goes with most colors. And I like this pink carryall and this black textured bag. They're funky and functional," Barbie said.

"I like them, too," Teresa agreed. "What about these stylin' sunglasses?"

"Now you've got the hang of it!" Barbie said with a laugh.

go shopping

NEW→

Bag It!

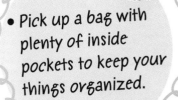

- Pick up a bag with plenty of inside pockets to keep your things organized.

- Choose short straps. It's easier and less strenuous to carry a bag when it's tucked right under your arm.

Fun in the Sun!

- Heart-shaped faces look best in small, slightly oval sunglasses.

- Round faces look best in square or rectangular glasses.

- Square faces look best in chunky round glasses.

- Oval faces look best in cat-eye or rectangular glasses.

Barbie and Teresa went out for a bite to eat and bumped into their friend Rosie.

"Wow!" Rosie exclaimed. "I love that outfit you're wearing, Teresa. Where did you get it?"

"Oh, this old thing," Teresa replied, blushing.

"I like your style," said Rosie. "Maybe we can go shopping together sometime?"

"Sure!" Teresa exclaimed. She couldn't believe that someone liked the way she dressed.

Barbie just smiled and winked at Teresa.

girly girl

Pink Road

cool store!

met cute boy

Fashion Blvd

fun cafe

Barbie Ave

fun store

xoxo

Friends Place

great shoes

At Lily's party, no one could believe how different Teresa looked.

"Is that you, Teresa?" asked Lily.

"Yes, it's me," Teresa replied with a shy smile.

"I love your belted miniskirt and that shirt," said Lily. "And that jewelry really makes you look stylish."

"Thanks," said Teresa. She was feeling more confident about the way she looked, and she became less and less shy. Teresa began talking and laughing with everyone. Soon she was the hit of the party!

DREAMY

Pretty!

♡ Totally ♡
Cool

Dress to Impress

- Prints and patterns as well as bright colors make you stand out in a crowd.

- Try something new—like mixing a short necklace with a long one.

- Try a sparkly top. It will make your face glow!

A week went by and Barbie didn't see or hear from Teresa. Then Barbie saw Teresa shopping with Lily.

"Hey, guys," Barbie called.

"Hi, Barbie," Teresa said awkwardly. "Sorry I haven't called you, but I've been kind of busy. We can't stop now, but why don't we meet at Justin's Restaurant on Friday for dinner?"

I wonder why Teresa is acting so strange, Barbie thought. *Is she so popular that she doesn't have time for me?*

So Cute

Sassy

That Friday, Barbie put on her favorite jeans and a flowery top and headed over to Justin's Restaurant.

"Surprise!" a crowd yelled when Barbie walked through the door. It was all her friends!

"What's this about?" asked Barbie.

"I just wanted to thank you for helping me find my style, so I threw you this party," Teresa explained. "Sorry I haven't been around much, but I've been party planning."

"So that's why I haven't heard from you!" Barbie said with a laugh. "I thought you had forgotten me."

"No way!" Teresa cried. "How could I forget my cool and casual fashion teacher?"